THE AMERICAN GIRLS

17 64

KAYA, an adventurous Nez Perce girl whose deep love
for horses and respect for nature nourish her spirit

17 74

FELICITY, a spunky, spritely colonial girl,
full of energy and independence

18 24

JOSEFINA, an Hispanic girl whose heart and
hopes are as big as the New Mexico sky

18 54

KIRSTEN, a pioneer girl of strength and
spirit who settles on the frontier

18 64

ADDY, a courageous girl determined to be
free in the midst of the Civil War

19  04

SAMANTHA, a bright Victorian beauty, an
orphan raised by her wealthy grandmother

19 34

KIT, a clever, resourceful girl facing the
Great Depression with spirit and determination

19  44

MOLLY, who schemes and dreams on the
home front during World War Two

1824
HAPPY BIRTHDAY, JOSEFINA!
A Springtime Story

BY VALERIE TRIPP

ILLUSTRATIONS JEAN-PAUL TIBBLES

VIGNETTES SUSAN MCALILEY

American Girl®

Visit our Web site at **americangirl.com**

Printed in China.
02 03 04 05 06 LEO 10 9 8 7 6

The American Girls Collection®, Josefina®, Josefina Montoya®, and American Girl®
are registered trademarks of Pleasant Company.

PERMISSIONS & PICTURE CREDITS
Grateful acknowledgment is made to Enrique R. Lamadrid for permission to reprint the verse on
p. 55, adapted from *"Versos a la madre/*Verses to Mother" in *Tesoros del Espíritu: A portrait in sound
of Hispanic New Mexico*, University of New Mexico Press, © 1994 Enrique R. Lamadrid.

The following individuals and organizations have generously given permission to reprint
illustrations contained in "Looking Back": pp. 62–63—Museum of New Mexico Collections,
Museum of International Folk Art, Santa Fe. Photo by Blair Clark (jar, mortar, pestle);
Los Angeles County Museum of Natural History, accession #1609-14 (baptismal gown);
Nuestra Señora del Refugio/Our Lady of Refuge by José Rafael Aragón. Museum of New Mexico
Collections, Museum of International Folk Art. Photo by Mary Peck; pp. 64–65—International
Folk Art Foundation Collections, Museum of International Folk Art. Photo by Blair Clark
(toy horse); Virginia Johnson Collection, #32203, New Mexico State Records Center & Archives,
Santa Fe (woman plastering); photo by James N. Furlong, courtesy Museum of New Mexico,
neg. #138858 (goats); *Zuni Indians* by Willard Leroy Metcalf, The Hyde Collection, Glens Falls,
New York; pp. 66–67—*Dancing on the Veranda* by A. F. Harmer. History Collections,
Los Angeles County Museum of Natural History, photo of painting by Seaver Center for
Western History Research, Los Angeles County Museum of Natural History;
Martinez-Sandoval Collection, New Mexico State Records Center & Archives (proposal);
photo by Jesse L. Nusbaum, courtesy Museum of New Mexico, neg. #61817 (wedding).

Cover Art by Jean-Paul Tibbles

Library of Congress Cataloging-in-Publication Data

Tripp, Valerie, 1951–
Happy birthday, Josefina! : a springtime story / by Valerie Tripp ;
illustrations, Jean-Paul Tibbles ; vignettes, Susan McAliley. — 1st ed.
p. cm. — (The American girls collection)
"Book four"
Summary: Josefina hopes to become a "curandera" or healer like Tía Magdalena, and she is
tested just before her tenth birthday when a friend receives a potentially fatal snakebite.
ISBN 1-56247-588-6 (hardcover). — ISBN 1-56247-587-8 (pbk)
[1. Healers—Fiction. 2. Ranch life—New Mexico—Fiction. 3. Mexican Americans—Fiction.
4. Aunts—Fiction. 5. New Mexico—History—To 1848—Fiction.]
I. Tibbles, Jean-Paul, ill. II. McAliley, Susan. III. Title. IV. Series.
PZ7.T7363 Hao 1998 [Fic]—DC21 97-33218 CIP AC

TO PEGGY JACKSON
WITH THANKS

Josefina and her family speak
Spanish, so you'll see some
Spanish words in this book.
If you can't tell what a word
means from reading the story
or looking at the illustrations,
you can turn to the "Glossary
of Spanish Words" that begins
on page 68. It will tell you what
the word means and how to
pronounce it.

Remember that in Spanish,
"j" is pronounced like "h."
That means Josefina's name is
pronounced "ho-seh-FEE-nah."

TABLE OF CONTENTS

JOSEFINA'S FAMILY
AND FRIENDS

CHAPTER ONE
SPRING SPROUTS   1

CHAPTER TWO
TÍA MAGDALENA   18

CHAPTER THREE
SECOND CHANCES   34

CHAPTER FOUR
RATTLESNAKE   48

LOOKING BACK   61

GLOSSARY OF SPANISH WORDS   68

JOSEFINA'S FAMILY

PAPÁ
Josefina's father, who guides his family and his rancho with quiet strength.

ANA
Josefina's oldest sister, who is married and has two little boys.

JOSEFINA
A nine-year-old girl whose heart and hopes are as big as the New Mexico sky.

FRANCISCA
Josefina's fifteen-year-old sister, who is headstrong and impatient.

CLARA
Josefina's practical, sensible sister, who is twelve years old.

TÍA DOLORES
*Josefina's aunt, who
has lived far away in
Mexico City for ten years.*

TÍA MAGDALENA
*Josefina's godmother,
a respected healer.*

MARIANA
*Josefina's friend, who
lives in the nearby
Indian pueblo.*

SPRING SPROUTS

Josefina loved spring. She loved the way it came swooping in like a bird on a breeze. She loved the way it woke the earth up from its deep winter sleep and made the *rancho* a busy, lively place. Baby animals were born in the spring. The sun stayed longer in the sky, and there were small green surprises here and there where things were beginning to grow.

Just now, Josefina had a surprise to share. She swung open the door to the weaving room and poked her head inside. "Tía Dolores!" she said eagerly. "Please, come with me. I have something wonderful to show you."

Tía Dolores looked up. The wind through the

1

open door fluttered the pages of her ledger book, which was on her lap. Josefina saw that Papá was in the weaving room, too. He was counting finished woven blankets, and Tía Dolores was writing the numbers in her ledger with her quill pen.

"Oh! Forgive me for interrupting, Papá," said Josefina.

"Well," said Papá cheerfully. "I'd like to see something wonderful, too. I suppose our counting can wait, don't you, Dolores?"

"Of course!" said Tía Dolores, putting down her pen.

Papá made a little bow from the waist and held out his hand toward the door. Tía Dolores swept by him, and they both followed Josefina as she walked quickly across the courtyard to the back corner.

"Just look!" said Josefina. She knelt down and lifted a handful of dead leaves. Underneath, skinny yellow-green sprouts were sticking up out of the soil. Josefina lifted another handful of leaves, and then another, and every time there were green shoots underneath.

"Sprouts everywhere!" she said. "More than ever before! Pretty soon the whole corner will be full of flowers."

"*Sí*, it will," agreed Papá. He sounded pleased. He put his hand on Josefina's head and smoothed her hair.

Tía Dolores knelt down, too. Josefina loved the way her aunt never minded getting dirt on her skirt or her hands. The sun shone on Tía Dolores's dark red hair as she bent over the sprouts. Josefina knew Tía Dolores was pleased, too. These sprouts were a promise kept.

Josefina's mamá had planted the flowers in this corner. During the year after Mamá died, Josefina had cared for the flowers as well as she could. Then last fall, Florecita, the meanest goat on the rancho, had torn up the flowers and eaten every last one. Josefina had thought Mamá's flowers would never grow again. But Tía Dolores had promised that they'd be all right. Now she turned and smiled at Josefina. "Didn't I tell you?" she said. "Flowers with roots as deep as these can survive a lot—even a visit from Florecita!"

Josefina grinned. "I'm still going to keep

3

Florecita away from them!" she said.

"Don't worry," said Papá. "Florecita will be too busy to bother your flowers this spring. She's going to have a baby very soon."

"Oh, no!" said Josefina, pretending to groan. "I hope Florecita's baby isn't like her. I don't think I could stand two horrible goats trying to bully me around!" Josefina laughed along with Papá and Tía Dolores. She used to be afraid of Florecita. She wasn't the least little bit afraid of the goat anymore, but she didn't like her the least little bit, either.

It was cool that night. Josefina was glad she had left a blanket of dead leaves spread over the sprouts to protect them. And she was glad she had a blanket of woven wool spread over her lap, though the family *sala* was warm.

Josefina and her sisters, Ana, Francisca, and Clara, were sewing blankets. Woven material came off the loom in narrow strips, which had to be sewn together to make one wide blanket. Josefina made her stitches strong and straight. All the sisters were good at sewing blankets. They'd sewn many since the fall.

Tía Dolores was adding numbers in her ledger. After a while, she paused and asked, "Josefina, your birthday is coming soon, isn't it?"

"Sí," said Josefina. "I was born on March nineteenth, the feast of San José."

"When Mamá was alive, we always had a celebration," said Francisca. She was Josefina's second oldest sister, and she loved parties.

"Well, I think we should have one this year, too," said Tía Dolores.

The sisters looked up, delighted.

"After all, we'll have several things to celebrate," Tía Dolores went on. "It's the feast of San José. Josefina will be ten. Spring will be here. And . . ." Tía Dolores smiled as she said, "God willing, we should have quite a lot of new sheep by then. I've added the figures. We've made sixty blankets. That's enough to trade for ninety sheep— forty-five ewes and forty-five lambs."

"That *is* good news!" exclaimed Josefina. She and Francisca both put their sewing aside and went to look over Tía Dolores's shoulder at her ledger.

Ana, the oldest sister, murmured a prayer of thanks.
Clara, who was next to Josefina in age, calmly
continued to sew.

"It's good," said Clara. "But it doesn't mean we
can stop making blankets. We'll need them to trade
for *more* sheep."

"Oh, baa, baa, baa," Francisca bleated at Clara.
"Don't be so tiresome! We all know that ninety
sheep aren't enough to replace the hundreds that
Papá lost in the flood last fall. But it's a good start!
I think we should be very proud of ourselves. Sixty
blankets is a lot. I know I worked hard on them."

Ana, Clara, and Josefina glanced at each other
and then burst out laughing. Francisca complained
more than anyone else about working on the
blankets. Now she made it sound as if she'd been
responsible for them all!

At first, Francisca scowled at her sisters'
laughter. But in a moment she was laughing at
herself along with them. "All right, all right," she
admitted grudgingly. "The rest of you worked
hard, too."

"We might not have *any* blankets to trade if it
weren't for Tía Dolores," said Josefina. "It was her

idea to turn blankets into sheep."

All the sisters nodded and looked at their aunt with fondness. After the terrible loss of the sheep, Tía Dolores had suggested that she and the sisters and other workers on the rancho weave the wool they already had into blankets and trade them for sheep. Now, just when spring lambs were being born, they had sixty blankets to turn into sheep!

"Papá will be pleased," said Ana.

"When do you think he'll go to the *pueblo* to trade the blankets for Esteban Durán's sheep?" asked Josefina. Esteban, Papá's great friend, was a Pueblo Indian.

pueblo

"Soon," said Tía Dolores. She smiled over her shoulder at Josefina. "Maybe you'd like to go with him." Tía Dolores knew that Josefina loved to go to the pueblo and see her friend Mariana, who was Esteban's granddaughter.

"May I find Papá right now and ask him?" Josefina said.

"Sí," said Tía Dolores, who always understood Josefina's eagerness. "Go. Wrap your *rebozo* around you. It's chilly."

"*Gracias!*" said Josefina. She gave Tía Dolores a quick hug and pulled her rebozo up over her head. She was just about to hurry out the door when an idea stopped her. "Tía Dolores," she said. "Won't you come with me? You should be the one to tell Papá about the blankets and the sheep."

Tía Dolores started to say no, but Ana and Francisca chimed together, saying, "Go on. It *is* your news to tell."

"Very well," laughed Tía Dolores. She put her sewing aside, took Josefina's hand, and together they went out into the cool spring night.

They found Papá in the goats' pen. He was sitting next to one of the goats with a lantern at his side. He glanced up when they came in, but he didn't say anything.

"Papá," Josefina began excitedly. "Tía Dolores has good news for . . ." Josefina stopped. She realized that the goat next to Papá was Florecita. But she had never seen Florecita like this. The goat was lying on her side, hardly breathing. Her eyes were shut. "Papá," asked Josefina, "what's wrong?"

"Florecita had her baby tonight," said Papá. "But she's too weak to nurse it. I don't think she'll live."

Josefina looked down at her old enemy, Florecita. Living on a rancho, Josefina had seen many animals die. She knew better than to think of the animals as anything more than useful and valuable property. Still, as she looked at Florecita— the goat who had bullied her and poked her and torn up Mamá's flowers—somehow she just couldn't help feeling sorry. "Can't we do anything?" she asked Papá.

"I don't think so," said Papá.

Josefina let go of Tía Dolores's hand and knelt next to Papá. She stroked Florecita's side, but the goat didn't move or open her eyes. Her breathing grew slower and slower until at last it stopped. Florecita was dead.

Josefina sighed. "Poor Florecita," she said softly. Then she remembered something important. She turned to Papá. "Where is Florecita's baby?" she asked.

Papá lifted his *sarape.* Cradled in his arm was a tiny goat.

"Oh!" gasped Josefina, pulling in her breath. Tía Dolores gasped, too, and sank down on her knees behind Josefina.

9

Very gently, Josefina reached out and touched the goat's silky little ear. The goat turned her head and nuzzled the palm of Josefina's hand. "Oh," Josefina said again. The goat opened her eyes and Josefina had to smile, because her yellow eyes looked just like Florecita's, but without the evil glint. Suddenly, Josefina knew what she must do. "Please, Papá," she asked. "May I take care of Florecita's baby?"

Papá's kind face was full of concern. "The baby is very weak, Josefina," he said. "It isn't easy to care for an animal this needy. I think you might be too young for the responsibility."

"I'm almost ten!" said Josefina. "Please let me try."

Still Papá hesitated. "You must realize . . ." he began. Then he stopped.

Tía Dolores put her arm around Josefina's shoulder. Then, in a gesture so swift Josefina thought she must have imagined it, Tía Dolores touched Papá's hand. Papá looked up at Tía Dolores, and Josefina saw that his eyes had a question in them. Tía Dolores nodded. She seemed to know what Papá had started to say, and she was encouraging him to say it.

Papá spoke slowly. "You must realize that there's a good chance the baby won't live, even if you do care for her," he said to Josefina. "Think how you'll feel if you become fond of the little goat and then she dies."

Josefina understood. Papá was afraid her heart would be broken as it had been when Mamá died. And for a moment, Josefina was afraid, too. But then she looked at the little goat and all her doubts fell away. "I have to try to save Florecita's baby, Papá," she said. "When any of God's creatures is sick or weak we have to try to make it better, don't we?" She held out her arms for the goat. "Please, Papá," she said.

Papá sighed. Carefully, he put the baby goat into Josefina's arms. She held the soft warm body nestled close to her chest and rubbed her cheek against the goat's fur. The baby goat gave one small bleat, closed her eyes, and went to sleep as if Josefina's arms were the safest place in the world.

"Take her back to the house," said Papá, "and keep her next to the fire. I'll bring some milk. She's too weak to nurse from one of the other goats. You'll have to teach her to drink." He stood up and looked at Josefina holding the helpless, sleeping goat. "She's yours to care for now."

"I'll take good care of her," said Josefina. "I promise."

"That's *Florecita's* baby?" Francisca asked. "She's such a sweet little thing!"

"*Very* little," said Clara. "Puny, really. It's going to be a lot of work and worry to make *that* goat healthy and strong."

"The poor motherless baby!" said Ana tenderly.

Josefina's sisters were gathered around her, staring at the baby goat, which was now awake in her arms. Tía Dolores poured the milk Papá brought into a bowl and placed it on the hearth. But when Josefina put the goat next to the milk, the little animal didn't seem to know what to do.

"Here," said Josefina. She dipped her fingers in the milk and then held them up to the goat's mouth. At first, the goat seemed too weak even to open her mouth. But then she sucked the milk off Josefina's fingers. "That's it," said Josefina. "That's the way."

12

Patiently, Josefina dipped her fingers in the milk again and again, feeding the little goat almost drop by drop. Josefina liked the tickling feeling of the goat's rough tongue on her fingers. She was sorry when the goat fell asleep again, before the milk bowl was empty.

"Clara's right. Taking care of that goat will be hard," said Francisca. "But I hope she grows up to be as big as Florecita, just not as mean."

"So do I," said Josefina, hugging the goat. "So do I."

That night, Josefina and the baby goat slept on a wide bunk above the kitchen hearth called the shepherd's bed. Shepherds sometimes brought orphaned lambs there to sleep because it was heated by the hearth fire through the night. The little goat slept curved like a cat, her legs tucked under her body, her bony

shepherd's bed

head resting on Josefina's hand. Josefina woke up often during the night. She wanted to be sure she could feel the little goat's heart beating and the warmth of its soft breath on her hand.

The little goat made it through the night. Before

13

Patiently, Josefina dipped her fingers in the milk again and again,
feeding the little goat almost drop by drop.

dawn the next morning, Papá brought Josefina a
pouch filled with goat's milk. He attached a rag to
the end of the pouch. Josefina held it to the baby
goat's mouth. After licking it once or twice,
the goat sucked on the rag and hungrily
drank the milk out of the pouch.

"Look, Papá!" said Josefina. "Isn't she clever?"

"Sí," said Papá. He stroked the goat's head with
the back of his finger.

Josefina thought the goat was *very* clever to
have figured out how to drink from the pouch. In
fact, Josefina believed that Florecita's baby was a
superior animal in every way—even if she *was*
rather small.

❋

The baby goat grew stronger as each bright
spring day passed. She seemed to thrive on warm
sunshine, warm milk, and Josefina's warm affection.
It was not long before the goat was following
Josefina around everywhere on her quick, sturdy
little legs.

"She's just like your shadow!" joked Tía Dolores.
And so they all began to call the goat Sombrita,

which means "little shadow."

Soon everyone was used to seeing Josefina and Sombrita together all over the rancho. Sombrita trip-trotted down to the stream every morning when Josefina went to fetch water for the household. Sombrita tagged along while Josefina fed the chickens, which made the chickens cluck and fuss. The little goat chased Josefina's broom as if it were a toy and sweeping were a game she and Josefina played with it. She dozed peacefully while Josefina worked at the loom, and bleated noisily while Josefina had a piano lesson with Tía Dolores. Josefina loved to look down and see Sombrita's cheerful face raised toward her hoping for a quick pat, a hug, or a scratch behind one floppy ear.

As Sombrita grew more frisky, Josefina had to keep an eye on her all the time. The rancho was a dangerous place for such a small creature. She might be kicked by a mule or stepped on by an ox. Josefina especially worried about snakes. Snakes were just awakening from their winter hibernation, so they were hungry. In the spring, a rattlesnake was quite likely to strike a baby animal like Sombrita and kill

16

her. Josefina kept Sombrita close by, safe from harm. She had promised to take good care of the little goat, and it was a promise she intended to keep.

CHAPTER TWO

TÍA MAGDALENA

One warm day, Tía Dolores, Josefina, and the sisters were planting seeds in the garden. Josefina used a sharp stick to make a hole in the earth. She dropped a seed in the hole, covered it with dirt, then patted the dirt in place. Josefina always liked to give the dirt an extra little pat, to encourage the seed to grow. Josefina and her sisters tended their garden with care. During the summer they'd carry water up from the stream every day to keep the earth moist. They'd pull weeds and shoo away pests. Then in the fall they'd harvest squash, beans, chiles, pumpkins, and melons.

"Oh, I'd love a big slice of melon right now!" said Francisca.

"Me, too," agreed Josefina. She sat back on her heels for a rest. The earth was cool beneath her knees, but the sun was hot on her shoulders.

"You'll have to wait until the end of the summer," said Clara. "We ate all our melons months ago."

"We were lucky to save as many as we did," said Ana. The same storm that had killed Papá's sheep had flooded the kitchen garden.

"We'll harvest all we plant today, God willing!" said Tía Dolores. She nodded toward Sombrita, who was bleating at the birds flying low near the garden. "Fierce Sombrita is scaring away all the birds trying to steal the seeds."

The sisters laughed, because the bold birds weren't the least bit frightened by Sombrita. The goat saw that she was the center of attention. She began to show off by kicking up her heels and bleating even louder.

"Who is that noisy animal?" someone asked. It was Tía Magdalena, walking through the gate. She was Papá's older sister, who lived in the village.

The girls and Tía Dolores greeted her politely. Then Tía Dolores answered her question. "That's

Sombrita," she said. Her voice was full of fondness and pride as she went on to say, "Josefina has cared for her since she was born. The mother died."

"We all thought Sombrita would die, too," said Clara, who was always matter-of-fact. "She was so weak and pitiful."

Tía Magdalena looked interested. She bent down and scooped up Sombrita. She stroked the little goat gently, and Sombrita settled calmly in her arms. Then Tía Magdalena looked at Josefina. Her soft brown eyes were warm. "Why did you decide to take care of Sombrita?" she asked.

Josefina didn't know what to say. "I . . . I didn't stop to think about it," she said honestly. "I just . . . I had to, that's all."

"Has it been hard work?" asked Tía Magdalena.

"Oh, no!" said Josefina. "I love taking care of Sombrita!"

"You have done a good job of it," said Tía Magdalena. She handed Sombrita to Josefina. "Sombrita is a fine, healthy goat."

"Gracias, Tía Magdalena," said Josefina. She was pleased to be praised by her aunt. Tía Magdalena was an important person in her family, especially to Josefina, because she was Josefina's godmother. She was an important, respected person in the village, too. Tía Magdalena was the *curandera.* She knew more about healing than anyone else. People who were injured or ill went to her for care, and she always knew just what to do.

Now Tía Magdalena turned to Tía Dolores. "Here are the mustard leaves you asked for," she said. "Tell your cook Carmen to brew tea from them and give it to her husband to drink if his stomach ache comes back."

"Gracias," said Tía Dolores, taking the leaves.

"Please tell her not to use it all at once," said Tía Magdalena. "I haven't many leaves left. Tansy mustard is usually blooming everywhere by now, but I haven't been able to find any yet this year."

tansy mustard

"I've seen some growing by the stream," Josefina piped up.

"Your young eyes are better than my old ones!" said Tía Magdalena. "Perhaps you'll gather some leaves for me." Tía Magdalena tilted her head and looked at Josefina as if she were considering something. "And perhaps when you bring the leaves, you can stay for a while and help me. My storeroom needs a spring cleaning."

"Oh, I'd like that very much!" said Josefina.

"Good!" said Tía Magdalena. She smiled, and Josefina blushed with pride and pleasure. How nice to have pleased Tía Magdalena!

The very next day Josefina skipped along the road to the village under a clean blue sky. She had a bunch of tansy mustard leaves in her hand for Tía Magdalena. Papá, Tía Dolores, and the sisters were going to the village, too. Josefina had left Sombrita behind under Carmen's watchful eye. Josefina missed Sombrita, but she knew the little goat would only be in the way today. In the morning, the men and boys were going to clean out the water ditches, called *acequias,* while the women and girls replastered the church. And in the afternoon, Josefina would be too busy to keep an eye on Sombrita when she went to help Tía Magdalena.

acequia

Most of the villagers had already gathered in

22

the *plaza* when Papá and his family arrived. They called out greetings. "*Buenos días!*" they said.

"Buenos días," Papá replied. "It's a fine day to work, by God's grace."

"It is," said Señor Sánchez, who was in charge of the water ditches. "Let's begin." He and Papá and the other men shouldered their tools and set off to work. Clearing the acequias was a very important springtime job. Later in the spring when the snow on the mountaintops melted, the acequias had to be clear of leaves and sticks and weeds so that the water could flow to the fields. Without water, nothing planted that spring would grow.

"We'd better begin our work, too," said Señora Sánchez. The women and girls agreed. They took off their shoes, rolled up their sleeves, covered their hair, and tucked up their skirts. Replastering the church was another important chore. It was normally done later in the spring. But the weather had been so unusually warm the past few weeks, the women were replastering much earlier this year. Josefina was glad. As she scooped up a handful of gritty mud plaster, she decided replastering was a chore that was fun.

"Watch out!" Josefina shouted at Clara, who stood between her and the church. Clara ducked down, and Josefina flung her handful of mud plaster at the wall of the church, where it stuck—*splat*—in a glob.

Clara laughed, saying, "You'll splatter mud all over if you do it that way." Clara was neat. She *pressed* her handful of mud plaster against the wall.

But even Clara was easygoing today, thought Josefina as she spread the glob of mud over the *adobe* bricks so that it was smooth and even. The

women and girls gossiped and chattered as they worked. The very oldest ladies sat in the shade keeping an eye on the babies. They called out jokes and encouragement to the others.

adobe bricks

Every once in a while someone would start a song and everyone would join in. Voices high and low, in tune and out of tune, rose up from all around the church.

Josefina liked making the church walls whole again. Later, she and some other children climbed up onto the roof to spread a new layer of mud plaster on it as well. Josefina loved the feeling of

Clara ducked down, and Josefina flung her handful of mud plaster at the wall of the church, where it stuck—splat—in a glob.

the mud oozing between her bare toes. It was exhilarating to be up high, closer to the huge white clouds and the brilliant blue sky. Josefina and the others shrieked with joy as they slipped and slid on the slick mud to tamp it flat.

"Josefina!" Clara called out. She was standing below on the ground, looking up, shading her eyes with her hand. "Tuck your skirt up higher in the back or you'll get mud on it and look messy at Tía Magdalena's this afternoon."

"And pull up your rebozo so that it shades your face," Francisca added. "Your nose is getting as red as a tomato."

Josefina looked down at tidy, sensible Clara and at beautiful Francisca, who was fussy about her skin. She knew that right now her sisters envied her. *They* were too old to be on the roof.

Almost ten is a wonderful age to be, thought Josefina, exuberantly slooshing her feet through the mud. *I'm not too old to slip and slide on the roof, and yet I am old enough to take care of Sombrita and old enough to help Tía Magdalena!* She waved to her sisters and cheerfully ignored their advice.

"Bless you, child!" said Tía Magdalena that afternoon when she saw Josefina at her door with the bouquet of mustard leaves. "Come in!"

"Gracias," said Josefina. She stepped inside and took a deep breath. Nowhere else on earth smelled quite the way Tía Magdalena's house smelled. It reminded Josefina of the way the corner of the back courtyard smelled when the sun shone strong on Mamá's flowers. But mixed in with the scent of flowers was the sharp, nose-tickling scent of spices and the musty, earthy tang of the herbs that hung upside down in bunches from the beams.

Tía Magdalena smiled when she saw Josefina looking up at the herbs. "You'd like to know how to use them, wouldn't you?" she asked.

Josefina nodded, wondering how Tía Magdalena had known.

"The mint leaves ease stomach aches. The pennyroyal brings a fever down. I use the *manzanilla* flowers to make a tea to cure a baby's colic," Tía Magdalena said, pointing to each herb as she named it. "And speaking of babies, how is your sweet

27

Sombrita today?"

"She's *very* well, thank you," answered Josefina, grinning.

"She's *very* fortunate to have you caring for her!" said Tía Magdalena. Her face looked merry. Tía Magdalena was much older than Papá. Her gray hair was streaked with white. But when she smiled as she did now, her expression was lively. And when she moved, her step was quick and light. "Now, we must do some work," she said. "Come with me."

Tía Magdalena led Josefina to the small storeroom at the back of her house. The ceiling was low and there was only one narrow window. But the room looked bright because the walls were whitewashed a snowy white and the wooden table and door frames were polished until the wood was a shiny yellow. More herbs hung from the beams in this room. Along one wall there were shelves lined with jars of all shapes and sizes.

Tía Magdalena tilted her head toward the jars. "Here's where I need your help," she said to Josefina. Her eyes sparkled. "Why don't we make a game of it? You lift a jar down from the shelf, look inside, and see if you can guess what's in it. I'll dust the jar, you dust the shelf, and then you can put the jar back. All right?"

"Sí!" said Josefina. She reached for the biggest, most important-looking jar of all. It was blue-and-white china.

"Oh, not that jar!" said Tía Magdalena. "It's empty."

"It looks very old," said Josefina.

"Indeed it is," said Tía Magdalena. "It's probably the oldest thing in this house. It's even older than I am!" she joked. "It's an apothecary jar. I don't know how it came to be in our village, but I know that it's been here for more than a hundred years. The woman who was curandera before I was gave it to me. She got it from the woman who was curandera before her. Long ago, I believe, there was a whole set of jars like it. That's the only one left." Tía Magdalena pointed to a smaller jar next to the blue-and-white one. "Let's start with that jar instead," she said.

Josefina took the smaller jar off the shelf and looked inside. "It looks like pumpkin stems," she said. "Could it be?"

"Sí," said Tía Magdalena. "You're sharp to recognize them." She dusted the jar as Josefina dusted the shelf. "There's nothing in the world better for a sore throat," she said. "You toast the pumpkin stem, grind it to a powder, mix it with fat and salt, and rub it on the throat inside and out."

Josefina wrinkled her nose when she smelled the inside of the next jar. "I think it's bear grease," she said.

"Right again," said Tía Magdalena. "You mix it with onions and rub it on a person's chest to ease congestion."

The next jar Josefina opened made her sneeze. "Oh, that must be *inmortal*," said Tía Magdalena, chuckling. "It makes you sneeze and sneeze and sneeze. The more you sneeze, the sooner your cold is gone."

Josefina enjoyed helping Tía Magdalena. Every jar had a story in it, because every jar held something that Tía Magdalena used as a remedy. There was dried deer blood to be mixed with water and drunk for strength. There was vinegar that was so strong it made Josefina's eyes water. It was used as a soak to stop infections. In another jar there was a terrible-

smelling herb that was used to soothe achy joints. Josefina guessed what was in most of the jars. But once she came to something she didn't recognize.

"I don't know what this is," she told Tía Magdalena.

"That's the root of a globe mallow plant," said Tía Magdalena. "I crush it and make a paste to put on a rattlesnake bite to draw out the poisonous venom." She handed one of the roots to Josefina. "Put that in your pouch and take it home with you," she said with a mischievous look. "And someday, ask your papá if he recognizes it."

globe mallow root

"Papá?" asked Josefina.

"Sí," said Tía Magdalena.

"Once, when he was a boy just about your age, he was guarding the sheep. He tried to scare away a rattlesnake by hitting it with a pebble from his sling. He missed. The snake got mad and bit him. Your papá killed the snake with a rock before he came to me for help. That was very brave, but very foolish of him! If you don't get the venom out right away, it can kill you." She shook her head. "I'll never forget the sight of him coming toward me, so proud of his own courage, and with that dead snake slung over his shoulders!"

Josefina put the root in her pouch and shuddered. She hated even *hearing* about snakes! But she liked to hear Tía Magdalena tell stories about Papá when he was a boy.

"Your papá was always too fearless and too stubborn for his own good," Tía Magdalena said as she dusted a jar. "And too quiet. But that didn't matter when your mamá was alive. She knew what he was thinking anyway."

Josefina was surprised at how easy it was to talk to Tía Magdalena about Mamá as they worked.

"Sometimes it seems so long ago that Mamá died," Josefina said. "Sometimes it seems like it just happened. And sometimes I'll see Mamá in a dream, and it seems as if she's still with us."

"Sí," said Tía Magdalena. Her old brown eyes seemed to see right into Josefina's heart. "That is how it is always going to be for you."

"Sí," said Josefina, running her cloth over a shelf to dust it. "And for Papá, too, I think. He's not quite so quiet and sad as he was just after Mamá died. It has been better for us all since Tía Dolores came. We needed her."

"Well," said Tía Magdalena, handing a jar to Josefina. "Perhaps *she* needed *you,* too."

Josefina wondered what Tía Magdalena meant. But just then, Tía Magdalena said, "I think it's time for a cup of tea, don't you?" And so Josefina didn't have a chance to ask.

CHAPTER
THREE

SECOND CHANCES

 When they were seated with their tea and some sweet cookies, Tía Magdalena said, "You've done well today."

"Gracias," said Josefina. "I was glad to help." She sipped her hot mint tea and gathered her courage to say what she was thinking. "I've really enjoyed all of this afternoon," she said. "And I was thinking . . . I was thinking that I'd like to be a curandera when I am older."

Tía Magdalena studied Josefina's face as she listened.

Josefina was encouraged. "Do you think you could teach me?" she asked. "When I'm old enough, I mean. I know I'm too young now."

Tía Magdalena thought for a while. When she answered, her voice was kind. "You can't simply choose to be a curandera," she said. "You have to know which herbs cure which ills, and you have to be observant and careful. But more than all that, you must be a healer."

"A healer," repeated Josefina. "How will I know if I'm a healer or not?"

"You'll know," said Tía Magdalena. "You'll know. It will be clear to you and to everyone else if you are."

Josefina sighed. "I hope I am," she said.

"You'll find out," said Tía Magdalena. "In time."

While Tía Magdalena cleared up after their tea, Josefina went back to the storeroom to finish dusting. All the while, she was remembering what Tía Magdalena had said. How she wished there were some way to prove to Tía Magdalena that she was the right kind of person to be a curandera!

Josefina looked at the big blue-and-white jar on the shelf and thought about how it had been handed down from curandera to curandera. The jar was dusty. Surely Tía Magdalena would be pleased if she dusted it as a surprise for her. Josefina stood on her tiptoes to take the jar off the shelf. She could reach it with only one hand. She tapped the jar to move it to the edge of the shelf so that she could lift it off with both hands and . . . CRASH!

The jar fell to the floor and smashed into a thousand pieces. Josefina's heart stopped beating. For a terrible moment she stood still, staring in horror at what she had done. Then, without thinking, Josefina ran from the room. She flew past Tía Magdalena, out the door, and ran away as fast as she could.

Shame, shame, shame! The word pounded in Josefina's head with every step she took. Josefina ran without thinking about where she was going. Faster and faster she ran, out of the village, up the road to the rancho, toward the house, until she came to the orchard. She climbed up into her favorite apricot tree. Its branches were thickening with buds, but there were no blossoms to hide Josefina. *How could I have been so clumsy?* she thought. *Tía Magdalena treasured the blue-and-white jar, and I destroyed it. Then I ran away! What a stupid, childish thing to do! Not like a girl who's nearly ten. I'll never be able to face Tía Magdalena again!*

36

Josefina clung to the trunk, and hot tears ran down her cheeks. She had been sitting that way a while when she heard someone say, "Josefina?"

Josefina looked down through the branches and saw Tía Dolores's face lifted toward her. Josefina felt as if all her bones had melted. She slid down from the tree right into Tía Dolores's arms and buried her face in Tía Dolores's shoulder. Then she cried and cried. Tía Dolores rubbed her back and let her cry. When at last her sobs stopped, Tía Dolores put a cool hand on Josefina's cheek and looked at her with sympathetic eyes.

"Your papá went to Tía Magdalena's house to walk home with you," said Tía Dolores. "She told him what happened, and he told me."

"Is Tía Magdalena angry?" asked Josefina. "And Papá, too?"

Tía Dolores smoothed Josefina's hair and said, "They're sad and . . ."

"And disappointed," Josefina finished for her. Roughly, Josefina wiped the tears off her cheeks. "I broke Tía Magdalena's most precious jar. Then I made it worse by running away. I ruined everything."

"Everything?" asked Tía Dolores.

Josefina was so ashamed and miserable she could hardly speak. "I was hoping Tía Magdalena would teach me to be a curandera when I am old enough," Josefina said. "Now she won't want to."

"Ah, I see," said Tía Dolores. "Can you tell me why you want to be a curandera?"

"It's hard to explain," said Josefina. She put her hand on her pouch and felt the root Tía Magdalena had given her. "I like helping people feel better. And I've . . . I've always wondered if there's a reason why Mamá chose Tía Magdalena to be my godmother. Maybe Mamá hoped I'd be a curandera."

"You mean, maybe she had the same hope for you that you have for yourself," said Tía Dolores. She hugged Josefina and said, "You know what you must do right now, don't you?"

"Sí," said Josefina. "Sweep up the mess I made, and apologize to Tía Magdalena."

"And you must ask her to give you a second chance," said Tía Dolores.

Josefina sighed hopelessly.

Tía Dolores bent down so that her eyes were level with Josefina's. "Spring is the season for second chances," she said. "Didn't your mamá's flowers sprout again? Didn't Sombrita get another chance to live when you promised to take care of her?" Tía Dolores smiled. "We're all given second chances. We just have to be brave enough to take them."

Josefina hugged Tía Dolores. She hoped Tía Dolores was right. Oh, if Tía Magdalena would give her a second chance, she would be so grateful!

Tía Magdalena had only one thing to say after Josefina apologized. "The jar cannot be repaired," she said. "But perhaps your hopes can."

Whenever Josefina made up her mind to do something, it cheered her. She felt awful about what she had done at Tía Magdalena's. But she wasn't going to let her mistake kill her hopes. She still wanted to be a healer. Tía Magdalena had said that it would be clear to her and to everyone else if she was. She was determined to find out. Josefina kept the root Tía Magdalena had given her in her pouch as a reminder to herself.

It was cold and rainy. It seemed as if winter had

returned. But finally, just the day before Josefina's birthday, the clouds brightened from gray to white and the sun shone. On that spring morning full of promise, Josefina set out with Papá and his servant Miguel to go to the pueblo.

Papá and Miguel were leading mules that were loaded down with blankets. The mules kicked up a lot of mud, so the blankets were wrapped in cloths

to protect them. The path to the pueblo wound its way next to the stream. The banks were dotted with wildflowers. In the trees above, birds sang loudly, trying to outdo each other. Josefina couldn't help feeling proud when she looked at the blankets. She had made some of them, and now Papá was going to trade them to his friend Esteban.

Josefina had another reason to be happy. She was going to see *her* friend Mariana, Esteban's granddaughter. Josefina had tucked her doll, Niña, into her sash because Mariana liked to play dolls. And of course she'd brought along her faithful little shadow, Sombrita, to meet Mariana.

The pueblo was five long miles downstream from the rancho, and after the first mile Sombrita

lagged. Josefina had to pick her up and carry her.
Josefina was relieved when the stream widened
and the pueblo seemed to appear all of a sudden.

It rose up between the stream and the
mountains. The pueblo was made of adobe
just as Josefina's house was. But it was
much taller than Josefina's house because
several stories were built one on top of
the other. Ladders led from level to level.

When Papá, Josefina, and Miguel arrived at
the pueblo, they entered its big, clean-swept center
plaza. There they were greeted by small children
and curious dogs. Sombrita was timid. She hid
her face in the crook of Josefina's elbow.

Esteban met them at his doorway.
"Welcome," he said to Papá.

"Gracias, my friend," answered Papá.
"May God bless you."

Miguel began to unload the blankets
from the mules. Sombrita stayed with
Miguel as Esteban led Papá and Josefina inside.
They sat down by the fire and almost immediately,
Mariana and her grandmother appeared with bowls
of food. There were little pies with fruit inside and

cups of hot tea. Mariana didn't say
anything, but she smiled shyly at
Josefina and her eyes had a welcome
in them. Josefina smiled back. Both girls knew they
shouldn't speak unless one of the grownups asked
them a question. It wouldn't be good manners.

As they ate, Papá and Esteban talked about the
weather, their crops, and their animals. Papá told
Esteban about the meeting the village men had held
to hear how much water each one would be allowed
to use from the acequias. Esteban told Papá how
much wool the spring sheep-shearing had brought.
Even though both men knew Papá had come to
trade, they didn't talk about it. To begin by talking
about business would be rude. Sometimes the two
men just sat together in a comfortable silence. They
seemed to have all the time in the world.

But Josefina was impatient. She couldn't wait
to show Sombrita to Mariana. Josefina tried to sit as
still as her friend did but it was hard. At last Papá
and Esteban finished their food. As Mariana and her
grandmother removed their bowls, Josefina admired
the way Mariana moved so gracefully in her soft
deerskin moccasins. Mariana wore a beautiful blanket

draped over one shoulder and belted with a woven sash. Her bangs fell to her eyebrows, and her dark hair framed her face.

"My friend," said Esteban. "Thank you for bringing the blankets."

"Thank you for accepting them," said Papá. "I've brought sixty."

"Good," said Esteban. "When the sheep are old enough, I'll drive them to your rancho."

Papá nodded. This was the way he and Esteban had always traded. Nothing was written. Esteban's spoken promise was enough. Papá said that his family and Esteban's family had always respected each other and traded with each other fairly.

Josefina knew that this summer both Papá and Esteban were going to trade for the first time with the *americanos* who came to Santa Fe from the United States. Papá planned to trade mules, and Esteban would trade the blankets that Josefina and Papá had brought to him today.

"I hope trading with the americanos will be a good thing," Papá said.

Esteban nodded to show that he shared Papá's hope.

Then Mariana caught her grandfather's eye and he smiled. Both Josefina and Mariana knew that was a sign that they could go. They stood up eagerly and hurried outside into the sunshine. Josefina picked up Sombrita and held her to face Mariana. "This is my Sombrita," she said. "We call her that because she follows me like a shadow wherever I go."

"Oh!" sighed Mariana. Her eyes were wide with delight. She scratched Sombrita behind her ear, just where the little goat liked it best. "Will Sombrita follow us to the stream?" Mariana asked.

"Of course!" said Josefina. "Watch!"

As Josefina and Mariana walked toward the stream, they peeked over their shoulders from time to time and shared a giggle at the sight of Sombrita following right on their heels. When they reached the stream, the girls found a sunny spot to play. Sombrita curled up in the warm grass and went to sleep. Josefina took her doll, Niña, out of her sash. Mariana had a doll too, made out of cornhusks. The

girls pretended that their dolls were sisters. They made necklaces for them out of tiny wildflowers, and boats from curves of bark.

The girls pretended that their dolls were sisters. They made necklaces for them out of tiny wildflowers, and boats from curves of bark.

They had just launched their boats in the
stream when suddenly Josefina stood up. "Where
is Sombrita?" she asked Mariana. "I don't see her."

Mariana stood up, too. The girls shaded their
eyes and looked all around. But the little black-and-
white goat was nowhere to be seen. "We'll have to
look for her," said Josefina. "She can't have gone very
far." She tucked Niña into her sash and Mariana
picked up her doll, and they walked along the
narrow footpath that led downstream. Josefina
hoped they were going in the right direction. She
could still see the pueblo behind them, but it seemed
to shrink smaller with every step they took. Both
girls knew they should not be so far from the pueblo,
but they *had* to find little Sombrita. They couldn't
stop. The farther they went, the faster they walked,
and the more worried they both became.

Neither girl said anything for a long while.
Then Josefina spoke as if she were thinking aloud.
"Sombrita's not lost," she said, trying not to sound
shaky. "She's not lost until we stop trying to find her."

With anxious steps, the girls kept going. Just
after they'd passed around the next bend in the
path, Josefina squinted. She thought she saw

something black and white in the grass ahead.
Could it be? It was! Josefina's heart lifted. "Oh,
Sombrita," she cried as she ran forward.

Sombrita didn't look at her. The goat was
staring at something else with friendly curiosity,
as if it might be a delightful new plaything.

When Josefina saw what it was, she stopped
short. All her relief turned to horror. Between her
and the little goat was a huge rattlesnake.

Josefina swallowed hard. She felt sweat on her
forehead and an odd trembling in her stomach. The
snake was coiled and ready to strike. Josefina heard
its eerie rattle. She saw its scary, skinny tongue
darting in and out of its mouth. She saw the snake's
beady black eyes in their sunken sockets. Josefina
bit her lip. The snake's cruel stare was fixed on
Sombrita.

RATTLESNAKE

"Josefina," said Mariana in a low voice. She saw the snake, too.

Josefina signaled Mariana to stay back. She had only one thought. *She had to save Sombrita!* Ever so slowly, Josefina sank down and picked up a rock. She held it out behind her to Mariana. Mariana understood and silently stretched out her hand to take it.

When their hands touched, Josefina whispered, "I'm going to get Sombrita. Don't throw the rock unless the snake moves, because if you miss . . ."

Mariana squeezed Josefina's hand, then she took the rock.

Very, very slowly Josefina edged forward. She

made a wide arc around the snake. Inch by anxious inch she moved next to Sombrita who, for once, stood still. Josefina stooped, gathered Sombrita in her arms, and straightened. Then everything happened so fast it was a blur. The snake gave a menacing rattle. Mariana threw the rock at it and missed. The snake whipped its head around, shot forward, and struck Mariana on the arm with its fangs.

"Mariana!" cried Josefina as she saw her friend grab her arm and stumble back. Suddenly furious, Josefina put Sombrita down and snatched up a rock. She threw with all her might. The rock hit the snake in its middle. With one last sickening hiss, the snake slithered away so fast it seemed to simply disappear.

Mariana moaned, sinking to her knees as if all the strength had gone out of her. She didn't cry, but her breath was ragged. Her eyes were shut tight.

Josefina bent over her friend. "Let me see your arm," she said. Gently, Josefina took Mariana's arm in her hands. She couldn't help gasping when she saw two tiny holes where the snake's fangs had sunk in. The wound was an ugly purplish color, and it was already beginning to swell. In her mind,

Josefina stooped and gathered Sombrita in her arms.

Josefina heard Tía Magdalena's voice saying, "If you don't get the venom out right away, it can kill you." Josefina spoke with urgency to Mariana. "We've got to get back to the pueblo," she said. "We need help."

Mariana tried to stand but dropped back on her knees. "I can't . . . I can't go that far," she said in a hoarse whisper.

Josefina's heart twisted with fear. She knelt down and something hard in her pouch thunked against her. It was the globe mallow root Tía Magdalena had given her. Without hesitating, Josefina took it out. She crushed the root between two rocks and spit on it to make it pasty. Then she pressed it against Mariana's arm where the snake had struck. She squeezed Mariana's arm gently to bring the venom up. Mariana whimpered, but she didn't pull her arm away.

Again and again, Josefina pressed the crushed root against the wound. Again and again, she pressed Mariana's arm. Again and again and again . . . Josefina knew she had to stay calm, but she had to fight against a rising feeling of panic. The globe mallow didn't seem to be working! Mariana's arm was still swollen and bruised-looking. Oh, how long would it take? What if she was using the root the wrong way? Perhaps she had misunderstood. What would happen to Mariana if the venom poisoned her blood? If only someone would come to help!

But no one came. The minutes felt like hours. Josefina was just about to give up and run for help when—oh, at last!—she heard Mariana take a deep, shuddery breath. Mariana opened her eyes, and color came back to her face.

Josefina said a quick, silent prayer of thanks. Then she asked Mariana, "Do you think you can walk if I help you?"

Mariana nodded.

Carefully, Josefina helped Mariana stand. Mariana looped her good arm over Josefina's shoulder, and Josefina put her own arm behind Mariana's back to support her. "Lean on me," Josefina said. Then she turned and looked down at Sombrita. "Listen," she said to the little goat. "Now you must really be my *sombrita,* my little shadow. Stay right behind me. Do you understand?"

Sombrita seemed to. She stayed close to Josefina and Mariana every step of the weary walk back.

Slowly, the two girls trudged along the path next to the stream. Slowly, they trudged up the long incline to the pueblo. Josefina knew they had been gone a long time, and Papá and Esteban would be worried. But she and Mariana could not move fast. Their tired feet dragged. Their tired shoulders drooped. They were only halfway between the stream and the pueblo when Josefina saw Papá and Esteban coming toward them. She had never been so glad to see anyone in her life!

Papá and Esteban rushed to the girls, and Josefina saw that their faces were tight with worry. Mariana said quickly, "A rattlesnake bit me, but Josefina knew what to do." She smiled weakly at Josefina. "Tell them," she said.

Papá and Esteban stared at Josefina, but she was too worn out to explain. Instead she held out her hand to show them the crushed root. "It draws the venom out," she said. "I had it in my pouch."

Esteban's expression did not change. His voice was very deep when he said, "Gracias, Josefina. Gracias." He lifted Mariana up. Papá, Josefina, and Sombrita followed them the rest of the way back to the pueblo.

Later, as they were walking home to the rancho, Papá asked Josefina to tell him the whole story of what had happened. So Josefina did. She didn't leave out anything, even though she was out of breath because she had to take two steps for every one of Papá's. They hadn't gone very far before Papá lifted both Josefina and Sombrita up onto a mule's back. After that Josefina couldn't see Papá's face, but somehow she knew that he was still listening hard to every word she said.

Josefina opened one sleepy eye. Could she be dreaming? It was not quite dawn, and yet she seemed to hear music. She sat up. Her sisters Francisca and Clara were gone from the room that they shared with her. Suddenly, Josefina grinned to herself. She remembered what day it was: the feast day of San José and her birthday.

Very slowly, the door to her room opened. In the pearly morning light she saw Papá, Tía Dolores, Ana and her husband Tomás, Francisca, Clara, Carmen the cook, and her husband Miguel. They began to sing:

54

On the day you were born
All the beautiful flowers were born,
The sun and moon were born,
And all the stars.

In the middle of the song, Sombrita poked her head around the corner of the door and bleated as if she were singing, too. Everyone laughed, and Tía Dolores said, "We wanted to surprise you with a lovely morning song, but I think someone forgot the words!"

Josefina picked up Sombrita and gave her a hug. "Gracias," she said to everyone, feeling a little shy at all the attention. "I liked it."

The morning song was only the first surprise in a day full of them. Ana made cookies called *bizcochitos* for everyone to eat before breakfast. At morning prayers, Francisca showed Josefina how she'd decorated the family altar with garlands of mint and willow leaves and how she'd surrounded the statue of San José, the saint Josefina was named for, with white wild lilies and little yellow celery flowers. Clara, who liked to be practical, surprised

Josefina by helping with her chores.

But when it was time to dress for the party, Clara had an impractical surprise for Josefina. It was a dainty pair of turquoise blue slippers. "It's about time I handed these down to you," said Clara. "I hardly ever wear them."

"Oh, Clara!" said Josefina, very pleased. She put the slippers on. They were only a *little* too big for her.

"If you're going to be so elegant," said Francisca, "you'd better carry Mamá's fan."

"And wear Mamá's shawl!" said Ana.

The four sisters shared Mamá's fan and shawl and brought them out only on very special occasions. Josefina swirled the shawl around her shoulders and looked behind her to see the brilliant embroidered flowers and the slippery, shimmery fringe on the back. She fluttered the fan and felt very elegant indeed.

The party table looked elegant, too. There was a beautiful cloth on it, and the family's best plates and glasses and silverware. Tía Dolores had made a special fancy loaf of bread. There were meat

loaf of bread

turnovers, and fruit tarts, and candied fruit that looked like jewels. But best of all, in the center of the table there was a red jar with one small branch of apricot blossoms in it. Josefina smiled when she saw the perfect blossoms. She knew that Tía Dolores had cut the branch from *her* tree—the tree she liked to climb. Josefina remembered the day Tía Dolores had comforted her next to that apricot tree. "We're all given second chances," Tía Dolores had said. "We just have to be brave enough to take them."

Soon music and laughter and happy voices swirled around the beautiful table. Friends and neighbors and workers from the rancho arrived bringing small gifts of dried fruit or nuts, sweets, or chocolate for Josefina. Esteban and Mariana brought a wonderful gift. It was a melon that had been buried in sand since last fall's harvest to keep it fresh.

When Josefina thanked her, Mariana said, "It's not much, but my heart goes with it."

Papá quieted everyone. "Today is the feast of San José," he said, "and today my daughter Josefina is ten years old. I'm going to tell you a story about

her." Josefina felt Mariana's hand slip into her own.
They both stood still, eyes shyly cast down, while
Papá told the story of the rattlesnake. Papá began
at the beginning and told everything that had
happened. He described the snake in such a scary
way it made everyone shiver. When the story was
finished, Papá called Josefina to him. He handed
her something that looked sort of like a shell. It
was rattles from a rattlesnake. "I've saved these
since I was a boy just your age," said Papá
to Josefina, "to remind me of something I
was proud of. Now I am giving them to
you, because I am proud of you."

rattlesnake rattles

Everyone clapped, and Papá leaned down to
kiss Josefina's cheek. Josefina thought she had
never in her life felt so happy or so proud.

Suddenly, Tía Magdalena was by her side.
"Dear child," she said.

Josefina smiled. She held out her hand to show
Tía Magdalena the snake's rattles. "I'm going to put
these in my memory box," she said. "They'll remind
me of the moment when I found out something
important about myself. I found out that I am a
healer."

Tía Magdalena smiled deep into Josefina's eyes. "Sí," she said simply. "You are."

Later that evening, when the party was over, Josefina and Papá walked to the goats' pen together. They wanted to check on Sombrita, who had not been invited to the party. Sombrita was fast asleep.

"It's unusual to see her so still, isn't it?" said Josefina. She and Papá smiled, looking at the peaceful goat.

"She's healthy and lively," said Papá. "She

might not have been, if you hadn't kept your promise to take care of her after Florecita died. You gave her a second chance at life."

Papá and Josefina walked back to the house. On the hillside, the flowering fruit trees in the orchard were lit by the moon, as if a pale cloud had settled on them. The night air was cool, but softened by the scent of blossoms. Josefina took a deep breath. She thought the air smelled like apricots.

"Papá," she said. "We're all given second chances. We just have to be brave enough to take them. That's what Tía Dolores says."

"Does she?" asked Papá. "Does she indeed?"

Looking
Back
1824

A PEEK INTO
THE PAST

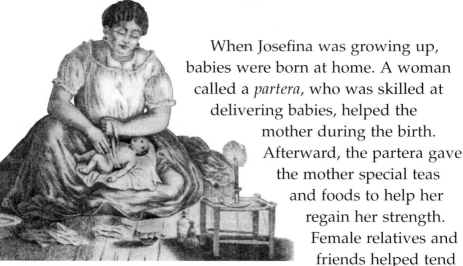

*A **partera** taking care of a baby just after its birth*

When Josefina was growing up, babies were born at home. A woman called a *partera*, who was skilled at delivering babies, helped the mother during the birth. Afterward, the partera gave the mother special teas and foods to help her regain her strength. Female relatives and friends helped tend the new baby.

In those days, mothers and babies sometimes died in childbirth. Fevers and diseases such as smallpox killed many people as well. When New Mexicans were sick or injured, they called on a *curandera* like Tía Magdalena for treatment. Curanderas knew how to make medicines from many kinds of plants. They received great respect for their healing skills and their wisdom.

*A **curandera** used plants like these to make healing remedies.*

Babies were baptized at the village church when they were only one or two days old. For this ceremony, the parents chose a woman and a man to be the baby's godmother and godfather, or *madrina* and *padrino*. Becoming a godparent was an honor and created a lifelong tie between the parents and godparents. The godparents helped teach the child and would take over as parents if the child was orphaned. Children usually had a special bond with their godparents, just as Josefina did with her godmother, Tía Magdalena.

A baby's baptismal gown from the 1830s

A baby received its name when it was baptized. Parents named children for religious figures such as the Catholic saints, angels, and people mentioned in the Bible. In the Catholic Church, each saint is honored on a special day of the year, called a *feast day*. Many children were named for the saint on whose feast day they were born—just like Josefina, who was born on March 19, the feast day of San José, or Saint Joseph.

Girls were usually given the first name of María, to honor Jesus' mother. Like Josefina, many girls were called by their middle name.

New Mexican children celebrated their saint's day instead of their birthday, or *cumpleaños*. On the saint's day, a child was wakened at dawn by the sound of the whole family singing a beautiful *mañanitas*, or morning song, often accompanied by a guitar or violin. Then everyone gathered at the family altar to pray, and the saint's statue was decorated with flowers. There would be treats such as hot chocolate, turnovers filled with fruit or meat, cookies, or bread pudding. Sometimes the family put on a puppet show or read aloud from a favorite book, and they gave the child gifts such as fruit, nuts, or a handmade toy. The child also had the honor of giving small presents to others. On Josefina's saint's day, she and Papá would give gifts such as chocolate or coins to all the workers on the rancho.

A hand-carved toy horse

Chocolate was a special gift on feast days.

For young and old, saint's day celebrations were a welcome break from the hard work of daily life. From an early age, boys helped the men plant and water the fields, harvest crops, herd animals, make rope, and repair farm tools. Girls fetched water, fed the chickens, and tended babies. They helped the

*Every spring, women and children gave the walls of their homes and churches a fresh coat of **adobe**, or mud plaster.*

Milking goats was a common chore for New Mexican girls. The milk was made into cheese.

women with housework, laundry, mending, gardening, and cooking. Children's work helped the family survive.

Children were also expected to be quiet and respectful around grownups, including their parents. To show respect when greeting adults, children kept their head and eyes down and their hands clasped in front of them, and didn't speak until they were spoken to.

New Mexican children had to work hard and behave respectfully, but they had fun, too. Stories, songs, riddles, and tongue twisters were favorite pastimes as people worked together during the day or rested by the fire in the evening. Children played with homemade dolls and toy figurines made from cloth, yarn, wood, clay, feathers, or leather. Boys played ball games and

*This painting shows Pueblo Indian boys playing a traditional game called **shinny**, similar to field hockey. Spanish settlers learned the game, too. It is still played in New Mexico today.*

girls played string games similar to Cat's Cradle. Popular pastimes from Spain included singing games such as *La Víbora de la Mar* (The Sea Serpent), which is similar to London Bridge, and guessing games such as *El Florón* (The Flower), which is much like Button, Button, Who's Got the Button?

In Josefina's time, young people received their First Holy Communion at age 12 or 13—much later than Catholic children do today. After their First Communion, they were no longer treated as children. Girls could wear their hair up and were

Girls practiced dance steps at home to be ready for the day when they were allowed to dance with young men.

allowed to dance with young men. At about age 15, girls were old enough to marry. Marriages were arranged by the parents. If a young man wanted to marry a girl, he would ask his father or uncle to write a letter to her parents proposing marriage and describing the fine qualities of the young man and his family. If the girl's family wanted

A marriage proposal from the 1820s

66

to accept the proposal, they would call on the young man's family after a few days or weeks. To refuse the offer of marriage, however, her family would give the young man's family a squash! This was more polite than saying no directly.

Weddings were festive events, with a dance and a grand feast that might last for days. Girls like Josefina were raised to be wives and mothers, and most married while still in their teens. The few who didn't—like Tía Dolores—usually spent their lives with relatives, helping to care for their families.

A New Mexican wedding in 1912. In Josefina's time, too, weddings were occasions for relatives and friends to gather from far and near and celebrate together.

GLOSSARY OF SPANISH WORDS

acequia *(ah-SEH-kee-ah)*—a ditch made to carry water to a farmer's fields

adobe *(ah-DOH-beh)*—a building material made of earth mixed with straw and water. Most New Mexican houses were built of adobe.

americano *(ah-meh-ree-KAH-no)*—a man from the United States

bizcochito *(bees-ko-CHEE-toh)*—a kind of sugar cookie flavored with anise

buenos días *(BWEH-nohs DEE-ahs)*—good morning

cumpleaños *(koom-pley-AH-nyohs)*—birthday

curandera *(koo-rahn-DEH-rah)*—a woman who knows how to make medicines from plants and is skilled at healing people

el florón *(el flo-ROHN)*— a children's game similar to Button, Button, Who's Got the Button? Its name means "the flower bouquet."

gracias *(GRAH-see-ahs)*—thank you

inmortal *(een-mor-TAHL)*—a plant called "spider milkweed" in English. It can be used to make a medicine for colds.

la víbora de la mar *(lah VEE-bo-rah deh lah MAR)*—a children's game similar to London Bridge. Its name means "the sea serpent."

madrina *(mah-DREE-nah)*—godmother

mañanitas *(mah-nyah-NEE-tahs)*—a traditional song sung to wake someone in the morning on a special day

manzanilla *(mahn-sah-NEE-yah)*—a plant known as "chamomile" in English. It can be used to make a soothing tea.

padrino *(pah-DREE-no)*—godfather

partera *(par-TEH-rah)*—a woman who is skilled at helping mothers during childbirth

plaza *(PLAH-sah)*—an open square in a village or town

pueblo *(PWEH-blo)*—a village of Pueblo Indians

rancho *(RAHN-cho)*—a farm or ranch where crops are grown and animals are raised

rebozo *(reh-BO-so)*—a long shawl worn by girls and women

sala *(SAH-lah)*—a large room in a house

sarape *(sah-RAH-peh)*—a warm blanket that is wrapped around the shoulders or worn as a poncho

Señor *(seh-NYOR)*—Mr.

Señora *(seh-NYO-rah)*—Mrs.

sí *(SEE)*—yes

sombrita *(sohm-BREE-tah)*—little shadow, or an affectionate way to say "shadow." The Spanish word for "shadow" is *sombra*.

tía *(TEE-ah)*—aunt

THE BOOKS ABOUT JOSEFINA

MEET JOSEFINA • An American Girl
Josefina and her sisters are struggling after Mamá's death,
when a surprise gives Josefina hope—and a wonderful idea.

JOSEFINA LEARNS A LESSON • A School Story

Tía Dolores brings exciting changes for Josefina and her
sisters. But will all the changes make them forget Mamá?

JOSEFINA'S SURPRISE • A Christmas Story
A very special Christmas celebration helps Josefina
and her family heal their sadness.

HAPPY BIRTHDAY, JOSEFINA! • A Springtime Story
Josefina faces a terrifying adventure, and her birthday
becomes a celebration of bravery—and second chances.

JOSEFINA SAVES THE DAY • A Summer Story
In Santa Fe, Josefina meets a surprising stranger—an
americano. He's funny and friendly, but can he be trusted?

CHANGES FOR JOSEFINA • A Winter Story

Josefina is shocked when Tía Dolores announces that she's
leaving the rancho. Can *anything* persuade her to stay?

◆

WELCOME TO JOSEFINA'S WORLD • 1824
American history is lavishly illustrated
with photographs, illustrations, and
excerpts from real girls' letters and diaries.